ALLIGATOR TAILS
and CROCODILE CAKES

For my parents – N.M.
To Hayley – A.E.

Contents

Hide and Seek

Crocodile was playing hide and seek
with his friend, Alligator.

Crocodile closed his eyes
and started counting.

"One, two, three, four, five, six..."

Alligator looked for a place to hide.
He found a big tree.
He stood behind the tree and
pulled himself up as tall as he could.

"Coming, ready or not," called
Crocodile. He looked
to the left.

He looked to the right.

He looked up and he looked down.

And then…

"Found you! Found you!
I can see your tail!" he sang.

"I want to hide again," said Alligator.
"And this time you won't find me."

So Crocodile closed his eyes and
started counting. "One, two, three, four,
five, six, seven…"

Alligator looked for a place to hide.
He found a space between two rocks.
He squeezed himself in and
made himself as thin as he could.

"Coming, ready or not!" called
Crocodile. He looked to the left.
He looked to the right.
He looked up and he looked down.
And then...

"Found you! Found you!
I can see your tail!" he sang.

"I want to hide again," said Alligator. "This time you really won't find me."

So Crocodile closed his eyes and started counting. "One, two, three, four, five, six, seven, eight..."

Alligator looked for a place to hide.
He found a hedge.
He wriggled under the hedge and
made himself as flat as he could.

"Coming, ready or not!" called
Crocodile. He looked to the left.
He looked to the right.
He looked up and he looked down.

13

And then...

"Found you! Found you!
I can see your tail!" he sang.

"I want to hide again," said Alligator. "And this time you really, definitely won't find me."

So Crocodile closed his eyes and started counting. "One, two, three, four, five, six, seven, eight, nine..."

Alligator looked for a place to hide.

He found an old barrel.

He climbed in and curled up. He

made himself as small as he could.

"Coming, ready or not!" called
Crocodile. He looked to the left.
He looked to the right.
He looked up and he looked down.
And then...

"Found you! Found you!
I can see your tail!" he sang.

"I want to hide again," said Alligator. "And this time you really, definitely, positively won't be able to find me. NO WAY!"

So Crocodile closed his eyes and started counting.

"One, two, three, four, five, six, seven, eight, nine, ten..."

This time Alligator didn't look
for a place to hide. He crept up
close behind Crocodile and
kept as still and quiet as he could.

"Coming, ready or not!" called
Crocodile. He looked to the left.

He looked to the right.

He looked up

and he looked down.

But he didn't look behind him.

"BOO!" shouted Alligator.
"I knew you wouldn't find me!"

"My turn to hide now,"
said Crocodile.

"Make sure you don't leave
your tail sticking out," said Alligator.

Crocodile and Alligator
Bake a Cake

Crocodile and Alligator were
baking a cake. Crocodile had
his grandma's recipe book and
an enormous mixing bowl.

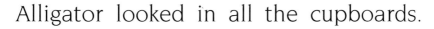

Alligator looked in all the cupboards.

"We need flour," said Crocodile.

"What's flour?" said Alligator.

"It's white, soft, and dusty,"
said Crocodile.
"And it's in a blue bag."

As he spoke,
a blue bag
wobbled and
toppled and
landed POOF!
on the floor
at Alligator's feet.

"Like this?" asked Alligator.

"Yes," said Crocodile. "That's flour."

Crocodile put four big spoonfuls
of flour in the bowl.

Alligator swept up the mess.

"We need eggs," said Crocodile.

"How many?" asked Alligator.

"Two," said Crocodile. "Two big eggs."

Alligator picked two big brown eggs
out of the basket.

"I saw someone juggle with
eggs once," he said. "Like this..."

SPLAT! SPLOSH!

Alligator wasn't a very good juggler.

Luckily there were two eggs left.
Crocodile cracked the eggs
against the side of the bowl,
opened the shells,
and let the eggs
drop onto
the flour.

"You must be more careful, Alligator."
"I will," said Alligator,
cleaning up the mess.

"We need margarine," said Crocodile.

"Where is that?" asked Alligator.

"In the fridge," said Crocodile,
"in a large white tub."

Alligator opened the fridge
and took out the large white tub.
He tried to open the lid.
It was very tight.
"Can you open it for me, please?"

Crocodile pulled
and tugged
and heaved
and... PLOP!

The lid shot off
and Crocodile
dropped the tub
onto the floor.
Upside down.

"You must be more careful, Crocodile," laughed Alligator.

"Very funny," said Crocodile and he picked up the tub. Luckily there was still some margarine left.

Alligator wiped up the mess.

"We need sugar," said Crocodile.

"I know where the sugar is,"
said Alligator. "I like sugar."

He reached up and carefully lifted
down the jar marked SUGAR.

"Be careful you don't slip…"
said Crocodile.

CRASH!

It was too late.

Alligator sat on the floor,
looking miserable, and covered
in sticky sugar.

"I don't think I'm very good at
making cakes," he said.

"You just need to be more careful,"
said Crocodile.

He weighed out what was
left of the sugar.

Alligator looked sadly at the mess.

"All we need now are
some raisins," said Crocodile.
"You can weigh them if you like,"
he added.

Alligator cheered up.
He weighed the raisins and
put them into a little dish.

"We add them later," explained
Crocodile.

"May I taste one?" asked Alligator.
"Just one," said Crocodile, who was
busy plugging in the electric mixer.

Alligator ate a raisin.
Then another one.

And another...

Then just one more.

"We're ready
to mix it,"
said Crocodile.
"Stand back!"

Crocodile switched on the mixer.

WHOOSH!

The flour and eggs

and margarine and sugar

spun around in the bowl

so fast it made Alligator dizzy.

"Is that really going to turn
into a cake?" asked Alligator,
looking at the creamy mixture.
"A delicious cake," said Crocodile.
He switched off the mixer.
"Now it's time for you
to stir in the raisins."

Crocodile poured
the mixture into
a big round pan

and put it into the oven to bake.

"Now we can clean up the mess,"
he said. "And when we've finished,
the cake will be ready."

They mopped

and swept

and wiped

and polished the floor.

Crocodile washed
the mixing bowl and the spoon
and cleaned the mixer.

"Mmmm!" said Alligator.
"I smell something good."
"I think the cake is ready,"
said Crocodile. He lifted it out of
the oven very carefully.

When the cake was cool,
Crocodile cut two huge slices,
and poured two glasses of lemonade.

"Scrumptious!" said Alligator.

"I'm good at eating cakes!"

"There don't seem to be many raisins in it," said Crocodile.

"May I have another piece?"
asked Alligator.

"Only if you sweep up the crumbs,"
said Crocodile.

"Just look at the mess you're making!"

About the Author and Illustrator

Nicola Moon began writing books for children seven years ago. Before that, she was a teacher. Nicola says, "When I was a child, hide and seek was one of my favorite games. I can remember helping to make cakes, too, just like Alligator."

Andy Ellis has written and illustrated lots of children's books. He also works on film animations for television. "Trying to make an alligator and a crocodile look friendly wasn't easy, but I hope the readers will think I succeeded!"

If you have enjoyed reading
Alligator Tails and Crocodile Cakes,
read these other Storyteller Chapter Books.